Up
Against
The MOB

ISBN: 978-1-961416-87-1 (sc)
ISBN: 978-1-961416-88-8 (ebk)

Up Against The MOB

F J DARE

Contents

ACKNOWLEDGMENTS

I would like to thank my family and friends,
who've inspired me to put my ideas
on paper to create this book.

CHAPTER 1
A BEGINNING!

It was the month of June in the year 1976; I graduated from high school as a young man not sure what to do with my life; I began to search for what life had in store for me.

This was the only question that was subconsciously asked repeatedly in my young mind at the time. What was I going to do for a living? What was the direction I should be going? To help me to make up my mind and to give me a little time to figure out my life challenges, I decided to enlist in the United States Marine Corps. Little did I know that day would effect my life in such a huge way.

It all started the day I arrived at the Marine Corps Recruit Depot in San Diego California for my basic training, and the day I met the person that would turn my life upside down some twenty-six years later. His name was Vincent Malone; I called him Vinnie.

I first arrived at the Recruit Depot on a green bus that pulled up and parked alongside the induction building. The bus was full of newly-arriving recruits. All of us on the bus were hot, nervous and scared; the sweat dripped from our bodies due to the lack of air conditioning on the bus. The driver was a small, thin man who also had sweat that dribbled down his cheeks, even though bolted on his dashboard was a small fan that rotated quickly, which tried to keep him cool. The small fan was no match for the hot weather. His small size was very noticeable to me, especially when he leaned over from his seat and grabbed a red handle that he struggled to pull back. After it had been pulled back completely the bus' front doors opened.

Now, with the door opened, the driver took his feet off the pedals, slid his legs around his seat, and placed his feet firmly in the center aisle, and then, he stood up. At that point he turned towards all of us and said,

"Stay seated until you're instructed to leave."

The driver was dressed in a Marine uniform with no markings on it. This informed me that the bus driver's rank was a private in the U. S. Marine Corps.

Once he completed his instructions to everyone on the bus, the driver proceeded down the three steps until he was completely off the bus.

At that moment, I remembered saying to the Italian man next to me, "What the hell am I doing here on this bus?"

His response was, "Just fuck'n pray, the shit we are headed for didn't even start yet."

Off in the distance, the sounds of men marching and the drill instructor's yells could be heard outside the bus as we all sat nervously waiting for our instructions.

Approximately three minutes had gone by since the driver left the bus, when a tall, muscular man dressed in a Marine uniform walked slowly up the three steps onto the bus; he stopped precisely at the head of the bus.

I could not believe all the ribbons and badges, which hung on his very clean, pressed shirt.

"My name is Gunnery Sergeant Watson," he said, oh so very loud and clearly that I believe everyone on the bus will never, ever forget it. "All of you pieces of shit, slimy civilians will now proceed to get the hell off this bus. I want you all to put your fuck'n feet on those yellow footprints alongside that fuck'n building." Quickly his hand pointed to the building as he continued to say, "You will not fuck'n touch me and I'm not going to move from this spot."

He then pointed to his feet with his two hands and his index fingers that pointed to his extremely shined shoes.

Continuing, he said, "Now get your asses off my bus, you have one minute to line the hell up." As I stood up, a line formed as I waited for the others to pass the drill instructor while they tried not to touch him.

It was at that moment in time many of us began to realize there was no way to get the hell by him. Getting by that man without touching him was nearly impossible. I was not going to attempt that so I wiped the sweat from my face with my shirt then began to climb out the windows as others tried to use the emergency exits at the back of the bus.

I remembered reaching over to my window, gripping the thumb locks at the top of the partly opened window. With both thumbs—one on each side of the window—I pushed in on the thumb locks; this allowed the window to drop all the way down. I placed my right foot on the seat then proceeded to squeeze my skinny body through the small, opened window.

The side of the bus was searing from the hot sun as it beat down on the bus's metal exterior. I could feel the heat as my hands walked my body down the side of the bus; I hung my body from the side by hooking my two feet on the edges of the window's frame. This held me there with my head inches from the blacktop.

I now placed my hands on the ground and released my feet from the window. It was at that time I began to feel all the muscles in my arms adjust for the extra body weight. I tucked my head in as I rolled away from the bus. Quickly I stood up, and ran like a scared rabbit to the footprints where I was ordered to line up.

I placed my feet directly on top of the faded yellow footprints in the same direction as they were painted on the blacktop. As I stood there waiting at attention, my body faced the building. All I could hear from behind me, were people being rushed off the bus as Gunnery Sergeant Watson yelled, "Faster, faster; get the hell over to those footprints you slimy civilians!"

However, everyone on the bus finally made their way over to the footprints. I don't think it happened in one minute though. It felt more like… well…lets say, like when I'm back home in Philly on a cold winter morning, waiting for a SEPTA bus, and I see it for the first time down the street blocks away. The time it took to reach me at the corner and open its doors, on a cold morning that feels like forever, but really it was only about five minutes. As we all stood there at attention, Gunnery Sergeant Watson said as he exited the bus, "From this time forward anytime someone in uniform talks to you, your answer better be Sir, yes, Sir or Sir, no, Sir. Do I make myself clear?"

"Sir, yes, Sir", we all responded. "I can't hear you," Watson said.

"Sir, yes, Sir," we all said in a louder tone.

That instant started the thirteen weeks of physical and mental hell that I thought would never end. Over the thirteen-week period, we were to be broken down mentally and physically; we were to be conditioned so that our bodies were at their maximum peak condition. Then we would be considered U.S. Marines.

At last, it was graduation day and time to get the hell out of the Recruit Depot and the town it was in.

CHAPTER 2
MEETING PLACE!

Graduation from Marine Corps Recruit Depot led me to my new duty station, however, my new location was still in the sunny state of California. To my surprise, one of my recruit buddies, Vincent Malone, was a new arrival there too.

Vinnie and I became buddies, the main reason being because we had recognized each other from that bus at boot camp. Once we became familiar with our new job tasks, like most people, we started to anticipate our liberty time, which in the military meant time off from work. That was when the two of us started to spend our off time at the non-commissioned officers club.

Vinnie was a big man; about six foot five inches in height, muscular, with black hair. There was no way he would be able to hide his Italian background, nor the fact that he was a ladies man. He was tall, dark, and handsome, and the girls just seemed to swarm all over him. Of course, at the young age of eighteen, we were all trying to become a ladies man. I mean all of us were young and in our prime, sexual peak.

It was so easy for him, I remember one night we sat in a bar in town, it was called Vinnie's Place. He liked this place because of its name and the big, red, neon-lit sign that read Vinnie's Place.

"This place has a great name; with a name like this, it can't be all that bad," was always his favorite way to describe it.

I haven't been in many bars at this point of my life so I remembered how overwhelmed I felt as we entered the bar. The inside was pretty cool. It had lots of white, Christmas-like lights used as a border around the shelves. They were used to help light up the bottles of alcohol stored on the shelves located behind the bars. There was one bar on each end of the building, with a stage in the center for the bands, which usually played in the evenings and all day on weekends.

That night as we sat at the bar, Vinnie drank his favorite drink a 7&7 and I was a rum and coke man. The smell of cigarette smoke filled the air and the counter tops were damp, sticky and smelled like beer. Vinnie, looking up towards the entrance, and with his eyes open wide he said, "Look at that," as the rock band played.

When I turned around and looked across the smoke- filled room, there was one of the most exciting looking women I had ever set my young eyes on, up to that time of my life. She had long, black hair that stopped around her ass, her hair was combed perfectly, not a one out of place. On her face she wore makeup around her eyes and cherry red lipstick on her lips. Not too much, just enough.

Her attire was very passionate; a black, leather jump suit that was skintight with a zipper up the front, which she had zipped up to about her bust line. Her breast size looked to be about a thirty-six 'c' to me. Every curve and line could be seen through that outfit.

When I turned and looked back at Vinnie, removing the drink from his mouth, he yelled over the loud music, "My dick is tingling. I need some of that."

"You go for it, Vinnie."

"What do you think of her? Why aren't you going to hit on her?" he yelled.

"She is hot, but a little too tall for me."

In the seventies, most women liked the guy to be taller than they were.

As the night went on, Vinnie would make contact with her about three times. On the last time that night, he was approached by another man who was getting pissed off at him as he relentlessly tried to hit on her. Both of them were drunk and the first fight of the night broke out and was on.

The man tried to punch Vinnie with a right hook; Vinnie ducked and came up in full-speed as he punched the man in the face. The poor guy made a mistake that night, and I'm sure he will never forget the beating he took. Even when Vinnie put him on the ground, he did not stop, he continued to punch him. The blood from the man's face covered Vinnie's hands.

Within minutes, two other men from the crowd jumped on Vinnie. As he began to mix it up with the two men, I went to his defense to even up the sides. Yes! Two against three was even that night because we had no problem overpowering them; we kicked their asses. After the fight Vinnie and I looked over to the girl in the black, leather jump suit; all she did was smile at him.

When we walked out the doors, we noticed an alley on the side of the building, and with the sounds of police sirens in the background, we decided to duck into the alley in an effort to stay out of sight.

While we walked through the alley, our friendship continued to build between us with Vinnie saying, "Thanks for helping me."

I said to Vinnie as I kicked a soda can and began to listen to it as it rolled down the alley as we walked, "Well, you did great on your own, but when he got help I thought you should have help too."

Just then he asked, "Did you see her smile at me when we left the bar?"

"Yes I did", I responded, as I continued to kick the soda can down the alley.

Months had gone by since that night in the bar and Vinnie finally did hook up with that girl. As he spent more time with her, I mainly saw him at work and not at the club. He began to hang out at Vinnie's Place in the evenings after his shift at work. He spent time with a new crowd of people.

I wasn't sure about the bar and was content just

hanging at the enlisted men's club on base where I met a women name Marge. Sex was instantly on my mind, but being friends with no sex was all Marge really wanted. She was a waitress at the club and didn't want to have problems in the work place. Although, in the back of my mind I hope someday sex would come into the relationship. Marge was a good person and we enjoyed conversing with each other when she had no customers to wait on. Tuesday and Wednesday nights usually were great nights for us to talk.

On the military base we all lived in buildings filled with bunk beds and we each were given a locker for our personal belongings. These buildings were known as barracks. Vinnie lived in one while I lived in another, three buildings down from his.

One night he came to my barracks looking for me. I had a lower level bunk in a barracks of about sixty men. I laid on my stomach with my eyes closed, but wasn't fully asleep.

I listened to the rain as it bounced off my half-open window, when all of a sudden I heard a clicking noise and a man voice that said, "Your money or your life." At that time I lifted my head, and turned it in the direction of the voice. To my surprise I gazed down the barrel of a forty-five caliber semi-automatic pistol; behind it, was Vinnie.

I said, as I stared intensely down the barrel of the gun, "Get that fuck'n gun out of my face or I will stick it up your fuck'n ass."

Just then he lowered the pistol and said, "How did you know it wasn't loaded?"

I replied, "I didn't."

"You got to be fuck'n crazy or nuts, one or the other." he responded. While he placed the pistol back in its holster he asked, "What are you doing tonight? Do you want to go to the bar for some drinks?"

"O.K., let's go."

I sat up on the edge of my bunk reached down and began to put on my shoes.

On our way to the bar we talked; I asked Vinnie, "Why do you carry a pistol?"

He really didn't want to answer and hesitated, but finally he asked me,

"Do you remember that girl at the bar?" "Yes," I said.

"Well, her name is Loretta, and some of her family and friends are in the mob; dating her, you will never know when you might need the gun," he said.

"How is it going between you two?" I asked.

"It is great and we are falling in love with each other; I think I found the women for me."

"No! With all the girls that want you, you're happy with this one?"

"Yes Frank she is the one," he said.

Just than as we walked up to the bar, I stopped and looked at the sign through the rain drops as they bounced off the window; the sign that lit up and read, 'Vinnie's Place.

"What's wrong Frank?"

"I haven't been back since the fight we had the last time I was here with you. What if they remember us?" I asked.

"It's cool, I'm a regular customer now, and they all like me, its okay," he said.

When I walked into the bar I noticed that the statement Vinnie made outside to me wasn't bullshit. When Vinnie stated, 'they all like me,' he meant it. Everyone said, 'Hi, Vinnie,' 'Hey, Vinnie,' or, 'What's up, Vinnie?' it was clear to me he was a regular now at Vinnie's Place.

Loretta was there at the bar and with a huge hug and kiss for Vinnie; I knew love was in the air. He had been on the level with me.

After a few drinks, Vinnie and Loretta had decided to head out to a party they heard about and asked me to go along.

"Sure, why not," I said.

The party was at one of Loretta's friend's house. When we entered the driveway I could tell these people hosting the party, also had the money. The house was huge, with one of the longest driveways I had ever seen so far in my young lifetime.

We entered the house, and as I glanced around, it reminded me of the houses you see in the movies. I remembered thinking to myself, for the size of this house, the party was a small one, but to me this was a big party. There were about seventy-five or eighty people at the house and everyone partied. People had drinks and almost everyone smoked; I remember setting eyes on some people as they stood on the back porch and toked on what looked like marijuana. Not that I was a genius, but the water pipe was a big hint.

When I looked at Vinnie, I could see that he was slowly being accepted into Loretta's family, along within the family business. Vinnie kissed one man's cheeks when he entered a room full of men, leaving me behind as the door closed.

As the night went on, people paired off and headed up to the bedrooms for some sexual activity. I walked out to the pool where there was a little bar with eight chairs lined up in front of it. I sat down in one of the empty chairs and placed my rum and coke on the bar. I could hear voices from the people in the pool, and a pot aroma filled the pool area when the direction of the wind changed. After that, it blew the smoke from the patio into the pool area.

As I took another sip from my drink, I heard a voice say, "Hi my name is Beth, what is yours?"

"Frank," I responded, as I held my drink up to gaze at the ice cubes in my glass.

"Can I sit here or is this seat being saved for someone?"

Then I looked over at the girl's face. She was a very pretty woman in a white bikini bathing suit with long brown hair, which was still damp from swimming. She proceeded to put her long, brown hair into a ponytail and then began to put on one of those light see-through bathing suit jackets, which matched her white bikini. After asking the bartender for rum and coke, she sat down.

"Have a seat," I said. Not sure how to open a conversation with her I said, "It seems like we have something in common already."

"Oh yeah, and what's that?" she asked. "We both like rum and coke."

As we talked, time seemed to go quickly; after two hours of talking about everything and really saying nothing, Beth asked, "Do you want to go to my room for a nightcap?"

"Sure why not!" I said.

Leaning over, she whispered in my ear, "And if you're lucky, you might get a good lay tonight."

CHAPTER 3
THE MURDER!

It had been three years since Vinnie and I arrived at our duty station and it was going pretty damn good for us. Although, he was deep into the family and more involved into the family's business; the deeper he went, the more money he seemed to make them. They mainly brought him in because of all that money he started bringing them; after some time, the family started to learn from Vinnie instead of the other way around. God he had gotten so damn street smart, it was astonishing.

The day we hoped never would come, finally came for me. Vinnie was upset, but at the same time was relieved it wasn't him. I received orders and was shipped out to another duty station.

I remember Vinnie saying, "We are going to have the biggest fuck'n party Vinnie's Place ever had."

The night of the party was anything but, normal. It started that morning, Vinnie and I went out to a tattoo parlor where we both received the same tattoo; a Marine bulldog wearing a helmet. Above the helmet were the letters, U.S.M.C. and under the pointed collar, the words "Devil Dogs."

"We will always be brothers," Vinnie said, to me in the most sincere tone I ever heard him use.

After the tattooing, we decided to have a beer and then get ready for the party.

While we had that beer, the girl from the party (you know, the one in the white bikini) approached me, "Hey Frank, what's this I hear? This is your last night in town?"

"Yeah," I said to her in a sad tone.

We had become friends and seen each other on and off since that night at the party.

"You were not going to leave without saying good- bye were you?" Beth asked.

"No! Aren't you coming to my farewell party tonight at Vinnie's Place?"

"Yes, Frank, I wouldn't miss your last night," she replied.

Just then, Vinnie asked, "What's the matter Beth, do you want to get one last screw in before he leaves?"

"Maybe," she replied, "what do you think Frank; one for old time's sake?"

"Vinnie, I think Beth and I are going to get my clothes from the barracks and then go to her apartment, okay?"

Vinnie laughed and said, "Sure, go for it. I'll see you tonight at Vinnie's Place."

Once at the apartment, we both talked about the times we had together.

"Holy shit, look at the time! We better get ready," I said, grabbing a towel and heading toward the shower.

Only minutes went by when I felt Beth in the shower with me. As I turned, she kissed me on my lips and grabbed my penis at the same time. After a little foreplay in the shower, we proceeded right there in the shower to have that 'one last good screw' Vinnie asked Beth about back in the bar.

Later that night, Beth and I entered Vinnie's Place. The bar was filled with people all chanting, 'Hi' to me, and, 'we are going to miss you!' Vinnie and Loretta sat at the bar when Vinnie waved at me to come over to him.

"Hey Frank, tonight you can't tell me you're not a regular here. Hey, by the way, you both look refreshed." Vinnie said to us, but was smiling at Beth.

He signaled for everyone in the bar to quiet down. "I'd like to make a toast. Frank, you are my good friend, almost like my brother; I love you and I will miss you and when you get the hell out of the Marines, I hope you come back and look us all up."

Just then I felt a tug as Beth pushed me onto the stage and said, "Go ahead, say something."

As I stood in the middle of the stage holding up my rum and coke, I said, "Thanks Vinnie and everyone here tonight."

Moving my head from side to side in an effort to scan the crowd through the heavy smoke-filled room, I continued, "All of you are good people; some of you I call friends; even when I'm far away, you will all still be in my heart. Thanks everyone, and drink up."

As I approached Beth, she wrapped her arms around me gave me a huge hug and kissed me on the lips.

"Great job Frank," she said.

At the end of the night, I glanced at the front entrance and watched Vinnie and Loretta as they walked out the front door.

"Beth! Do you believe they forgot to say a final good-bye to me? Let's go I have to give them a final good-bye," I said, while we pushed our way through the crowd to the front door.

Vinnie and Loretta started to walk unsteadily down the alley towards his car. The alley wasn't completely dark; there were some pole lights that lit up a few parking spaces. That is where he liked to park his car.

Suddenly, the guy Vinnie had the fight with three years ago approached them. From time to time over the last three years, he made contact with Vinnie.

Loretta yelled, "Paul, will you just leave us alone?"Paul always pissed at their relationship, but had never gone to this extreme before; this time he walked up to them with a gun.

"I can't understand how someone like you can steal my girl and be taken into the family in such a short period of time. I fuck'n hate you, Vinnie, and you must die."

Just then, Paul squeezed the trigger; as the gun went off, his unsteady hand shuddered to the left; instead of the bullet hitting Vinnie, it hit Loretta in the stomach, and down she went. "You mother fucker!!" yelled Vinnie, as they wrestled each other to the ground.

Vinnie beat Paul until he stopped moving, just like before. When he finally stopped punching, he took Loretta into his arms.

While all this was happening in the alley, Beth and I made it out the front door of the bar. Hearing

where the gunshot came from, down the alley we ran. When we arrived, Vinnie was at Loretta's side still holding her in his arms and began to yell at the man, but I interrupted him.

"Vinnie what happened?" I screamed.

"Loretta's dead and that fuck'n ass over there killed her!" Vinnie yelled. "I'm going to kill you!"

After laying Loretta on the ground very gently, he stood up staring at the almost lifeless man on the ground.

With fire-blazed eyes, he yelled, "You mother fucker; you mother fucker! You wanted to kill me! Well you just fucked up; you missed me and killed Loretta! Now you are fuck'n dead! Say your fuck'n good-byes."

"Vinnie calm down," I said.

"Shut the fuck up, Frank, this bastard is dead," Vinnie yelled.

Without any hesitation, Vinnie took out the pistol from under his arm and placed it to the man's head. As he squeezed the trigger he whispered, "Say good-bye, asshole."

Bang! As a loud noise filled the alley, and blood sprayed from the back of Paul's head, I said, "Vinnie, you killed him."

"That's right, the bastard killed Loretta and I killed him."

"I'm scheduled to be on a plane very soon so I have to get to the airport. I can't get caught up in the middle of this shit. From what I can see, this was all self- defense," I said.

He looked at Beth and me with those fire-blazed eyes, and I couldn't tell if he was going to kill us too or let us go.

"Frank, go! Get your fuck'n ass to the airport I'll handle this shit, you two go now!" he said as he waved his gun at Beth.

"Thanks Vinnie, you can trust me, I will never tell anyone what happened here tonight. I love you man!!" As fast as Beth and I could we ran out of that alley for the airport, and never looked back.

Just as we appeared from the alley, the front door of the bar was partly opened and the sound of the band's music could be heard. As the door sealed closed the music faded off.

"What should we do?" Beth asked.

"Nothing yet, Beth, come on drive me to the airport, okay?" I whispered.

"Sure, Frank."

"I just have a plane to catch," I said,

As we rushed to her car, I placed a firm grasp on her wrist in an effort to speed her up as she followed behind me.

When we reached her car I opened the passenger's side door for her. There was a little squeak as it swung opened.

"Hurry, get in from this side," I said.

"Sure, Frank," she replied sliding across the seat towards the steering wheel.

She placed her key in the ignition, started the car, and drove out of her parking spot. Stopped at a traffic signal I stared at the people as they walked past the windshield.

"Are you okay?" she asked as the light turned green and the car began to move once again.

I reached over and grasped the knob on the radio with one hand and turned down the sound, as I swatted the foam dice that hung from the rearview mirror with the other.

"I'll be fine. You know I'm going to miss you. How would like to move with me?" I asked.

"Frank I can't just pack up and leave my present life. But with what just happened, it might not be a bad idea and …

Interrupting her, I said, "Stop this is my terminal."

As the car stopped I gave Beth a kiss, the scent of her perfume remained on my nose; after I got out, I stuck my head in the open window and gave her another quick kiss and said, "I understand, when I get to Philly I will give you a call."

Then, I shook the car door making sure it was closed, turned around, and walked into the terminal.

CHAPTER 4
UNFORESEEN OCCURRENCE!

It has been twenty-three years since that night in the alley with Vinnie and the death of Loretta; I never said a word to anyone about that night. The year was now 2002.

When I was discharged from the service it had been one year since the death of Loretta. Going back to California to hook up with my friends and start my life with them was on my mind. The relationships I created with some of those people were very hard for me to just forget about, especially the one I had made with Vinnie. I just thought to myself, that night was enough and didn't want to deal with the bullshit that might come up if I returned, so, I didn't go back.

However, I did eventually call Beth and she agreed to move with me; it was a great decision for us. Beth is now my wife and we have three children and even some small investments.

Life, I thought, was good, until one morning on my way to work.

That morning started out like any typical day, I woke up to a little morning foreplay and sex with Beth, and then came my usual morning shower. With my daughter in the local community college, my oldest son in high school, and the youngest son in elementary school, everyone in the house was awake.

Sounds of clock radios and water as it ran from showers could be heard throughout the house. After I gave everyone a kiss, the aroma of my favorite freshly- brewed coffee filled the air in the house and reminded me to grab my travel mug fill it with coffee and I started my journey to work.

The ride on most mornings took me about thirty-five minutes, except that day. About half-way through the drive to work, a big, black car pulled up to the side of me on the passing lane side and started to crash into the side of my car. Sparks flew through the air every time the vehicles hit one another. Along with the sparks came the loud sound of two metal substances hitting against each other. We were traveling about sixty-five miles an hour. The sounds I heard along with the banging of our cars when they touched each other, frightened me. I couldn't for the life of me figure out what the driver's motive was for his nonstop effort to attack my car. Suddenly, I had a hard time keeping my car on the road. The smell of rubber burning from his tires filled the air as the front quarter panel of the black car had gotten smashed into the tire.

I had no choice but to save myself so I turned the steering wheel into his car. Once I started to react that way, I could tell by the reaction on the other driver's face that he was surprised I went into such a strong defense mode. After about three miles as we weaved around the other cars on the road and my relentless attempts to get rid of this nut, our final contact tossed his car off the highway as it landed face down about thirty feet onto the shoulder of the road. The smell of gasoline filled the air.

I stopped my car, reached for my cell phone and dialed 911.

Other cars stopped to help me, and asked, "What the hell was that man trying to do?"

"I have no idea, except trying to kill me."

Once the police arrived, the first officer on the scene was someone I recognized. It was Bob; he was a previous security officer from my job's public safety department. That really helped to calm my nerves at the time; if it had been someone else, I don't believe that would have happened.

"What the hell took place here Frank?" he asked.

"This car tried for at least three miles to run me off the road."

With all the witnesses, he knew I spoke the truth. As we approached the overturned vehicle, the lack of body movement and with the amount of blood around him, it was very evident that the driver was dead.

After the police cleared the roadway and the dead driver had been taken away in a body bag to the city morgue, the police took me to their station, asked me thousands of questions and ran the dead driver's identification through the computer system.

When the results of the driver's I.D. came back, Bob walked up to me and asked, "How are you feeling, Frank?"

"I'm starting to feel better and calm down a bit more; who was that guy?" I asked.

"We were hoping you could tell us," he said. "Why's that?"

"The information came back blank, like the man never had an identity at all," he said.

"Shit! That sounds like something the government would do, huh!" I said.

"Or the organized crime lords," Bob's supervisor said from across the room.

I was totally unaware that my old buddy, Vinnie, from twenty-three years ago had worked his way up the mob's ladder, and I mean all the way up the ladder. Vinnie was now the godfather on the west coast.

I had never even given him a thought, when Bob asked me, "Do you know anyone in organized crime?"

All I said was, "Hell no, Bob!"

After the police allowed me to leave the station, work was out of the question for me that day. I just called my wife Beth and asked her to pick me up at the police station. We arrived at home sometime in the afternoon; I had a rum and coke in an effort to calm my nerves down even more. I then tried to explain what happened to me that day to my family. With my body still pumped up I explained the situation. It was difficult to do, and at the same time, all I could do. I was still stunned and I just couldn't believe all this happened to me.

CHAPTER 5
SECOND OCCURRENCE!

It has been about thirty days since that extreme ride to work, when the man in the big, black car tried to permanently put out my lights with his attempts to run me off the road. The police didn't find any information on that man and still had no idea who he was, or, where he came from.

Flashbacks of that crazy day always popped into my head and I believed it made me a little paranoid. At least I thought so. I just felt like people were watching me all the time, which kept me on the look out.

From time to time, I began to glimpse over my shoulder, until one day, at the local mall, I observed a man staring at me; and then he was gone; even as I continued to look over my shoulder there where no other sightings of him.

When I completed with my shopping and left the mall, I started to walk around the parking lot. As I looked for the car, this weird feeling came over me (this was because I didn't search for my car) it was a rental car I looked for while mine was still getting the repairs it needed from last month's incident.

While I continued to search for my rental car, I heard a noise blow by my ear, followed by the sound of car tires as they screeched. The sound came from a red Trans-Am that started to drive towards me as smoke from the car's back tires filled the air, and a dark cloud followed behind its path.

The car came closer and closer, I was then able to see the driver's face, and it was that well dressed man I had noticed staring at me in the mall. He had a gun in his hand. As he passed by me at a high speed, from the driver's seat, he shot through the already rolled down passenger window. I remembered seeing a flash from the pistol. All I could do was dive behind the nearest parked car.

After the car was gone I stood up. It was at that time when I heard a man groan and noticed someone behind me lying on the ground. When I approached the man it was clear to me that he was a young man in his mid-twenties and he had a gunshot wound in his left leg. Blood flowed from his leg and he screamed in pain.

I immediately asked the other people in the parking lot to call for help, while I began to slow down the blood flow on his leg.

"What's your name?" I asked.

"My name is Chris," he responded in a painful tone.

"You are going to be fine Chris, the ambulance has been called." I said.

At this time, I took off my shirt, using it as a pressure dressing. It quickly turned the color red from the blood and so did my hands, but the blood that flowed from the wound did subside as I continued to apply pressure.

People in the background yelled, "Ooh-gross"

When the police arrived, they began to ask everyone else what happened; they were not able to see us because the crowd surrounded Chris and me. The minutes felt like hours had gone by until the officer assessed what happened and was able to filter himself through the group of people. The ambulance had driven up to the scene almost at the same time the officer made his way to us.

"Hurry, hurry," I yelled, "this man has a gunshot wound in his left leg," I continued to scream until the medic's approached us from the rear of the ambulance.

The medic replaced me and stabilized the wounded man for transport. As the ambulance took Chris to the hospital, the police officer transported me to the station to clean up and have me answer more questions. While I washed the blood off my hands in the men's room sink, the door opened rapidly and a police officer walked in and asked, "What the hell happened out there, the crowd's stories vary."

"I'll tell you, I have some asshole out there trying to kill me and that guy, Chris, just was at the wrong place at the wrong time. He has no idea what's going on, but I do know one thing, I was being followed in the mall by the driver of that car and this is the second attempt on my life in a month!" I said very angrily.

As we left the restroom the officer was waved down by the dispatcher on duty, "I was asked to give you this by Officer Jones." he said handing a piece of paper to the officer.

"By the way, what is your name, Sir?" I asked. "Just call me Officer Peterson," his replied.

"Well, Officer Peterson, what's on the piece of paper?"

"One of the people in the crowd gave us the license plate number of the red Trans-Am that had shot at you, but he must have read the numbers wrong," he answered.

"Why's that?" I asked.

"That number isn't in the computer system," he said.

"What about the bullet from Chris's leg?" I asked. "With no hits on the computer and no pistol to

match the markings of the bullet up to, all we know is it was a .38 caliber that inflicted the wound."

"Oh fuck, not again," I said in amazement.

Before the officer said anything, I said, "Do you know last month I was run off the road and that man's information came up completely blank too?"

CHAPTER 6
THIRD OCCURRENCE!

It started to be very confusing in my simple life, and not knowing why these mysterious occurrences were happening to me, had begun to really get under my skin. Most of the people in my life were normal, everyday, working-class people that would tell me it's nothing, just a rough period in your life span and I should forget about it and go on with my life. I tried to get on with my simple life, but it wasn't easy, especially after about another thirty days. Another incident that happened to me began with what I though was the third attempt on my life.

The third occurrence started out as any other day at work. Then came an event that changed my normal day at work into having to defend myself against the people who were inflicting these 'out of the ordinary' occurrences onto me. Before I go into what happened the third time, let me say, because of a minor mistake this time, the identities of these bastards were finally revealed.

It was during my normal, daily functions as the Director of Facilities at a local college, when two strangers in the restroom approached me and they said, "Hey, are you Frank?"

My first thought was these two men were salesmen and the assholes weren't going to let me piss in peace.

As I stood at the urinal I pulled up my zipper and said, "Yes, I am. Can I at least wash my hands in peace?"

Both men were very well dressed and stood in front of me with one man to the left and the other to the right. Just then the man on my left began to put on his hand what appeared to be brass knuckles, as the second man placed his hand into the side of his jacket.

The man with the brass knuckles said. "Fuck you asshole."When he completed his sentence, the man using the hand that he placed the brass knuckles on, threw a punch it landed on my lower left ribcage, which took me to the restroom floor. Once on the floor, I could see a pistol being removed from the jacket of the other man. I had to ignore the pain and think fast or I was going to be dead.

My first thought was to take out the largest threat first, so I spun on the floor and used the heel of my left foot as a weapon; I then proceeded to take the second man's feet out from under him, by using a back heel kick across the back of his ankles. This in turn threw both of his feet straight up in the air. As that man landed on the floor only a foot away I could hear an "ah" sound come from his mouth as the air left his body and his pistol slid across the restroom floor. This gave me time to give the other man a nice left jab to his groin causing him to fall to the floor.

Now with the three of us still on the ground, I began to fight for my life and tried to get that pistol.

During the struggle for the pistol I began to yell at them, "You two assholes are going to fuck'n die."

As we still fought for the pistol my walkie-talkie attached to my belt came undone and also slid across the floor. Then to my surprise I felt this colossal pain in my right arm.

"Damn it," I screamed.

Then, for me, the most wonderful thing that could have happened did. I heard the sound of the men's room door swing open and two students walked in to use the facilities; as they screamed, my two assailants got up quickly, grabbed the pistol, and fled the restroom before a shot could have been fired.

Although the men and the pistol were gone, the enormous pain in my arm was still there along with the knife used to inflict my excruciating pain. With the knife stuck in my arm, the students continued to scream. The loud screams from the two young students is what really chased the men away.

Public safety responded to the scene to find me lying in a pool of my own blood.

"What the hell happened to you?" the first officer said to me.

"I was just mugged by two men," I replied.

"Dial 911," the first officer said to the second

officer, who just now entered the restroom. "Not a problem," the second officer said.

"Fuck it guys, just drive me to the hospital," I said.

It wasn't their normal procedure, but because of my influence they agreed.

The first officer replied, "Okay, Frank."At that time I reached for my work's walkie-talkie that slid on the floor during my struggle and said, "Frank to base."

A voice responded, "Go ahead Frank."

"Will you inform housekeeping there is spill in the first floor men's room that needs immediate clean up?"

Again, over my walkie-talkie came a voice that said, "10-4; could you tell us what type of spill?"

"A blood spill." I replied.

The first officer spoke again, "Christ, Frank, even with a knife in your arm you are still thinking about work."

I replied, "I know sad isn't it... I need to get a life." Once at the hospital I kept repeating to the local township police officer, "We need to get fingerprints off of this knife so please make sure the evidence doesn't get contaminated."

The break I needed was finally here, a fingerprint on the knife came back from the police department's computer. It was a man from the west coast mob named Rick Salmon (over the years Rick's fondness for brass knuckles, helped him to achieve the nickname of brassy).

With all this information the officer asked me, "Why would a gangster, from the west coast, be after you?"

"I don't know, but I am going to find out and you can take that to the bank."

CHAPTER 7
GATHERING THE FACTS!

Now that I received a small piece of the puzzle, it was time for me to attempt to make somesense out of this mysterious part of my life, along with the astonishing occurrences that seemed to want to be an unwilling part of my life.

To do this, I had to get all the background information I could about the man who wore those brass knuckles.

The only information that had been known to me this far was his name, Rick Salmon, and the fact that he had dealings with the west coast mob.

I became totally consumed with the mystery happening to me, I took the information I had to the neighborhood library and preceded to find everything I could possibly find out about Rick Salmon. I checked on the Internet and in the old newspaper clippings just trying to find something. Bearing in mind all the information I gathered, I began to feel as if I knew him and started calling him Brassy myself. Brassy had been a busy man on the west coast as a made man for the mob. The significant news came when I discovered who the top man in the west coast mafia was.

"Holy shit," I yelled as I read the facts on the computer.

Whispers of, "Quiet," came from the people two tables down, as they looked at me in a strange way for the noise I made in the library.

That's right, my old Marine Corp buddy, Vincent Malone, was now the godfather. Not only that, he was also being indicted on racketeering and murder charges.

As I read one of the news clippings it quoted Vinnie saying, 'I didn't kill anyone.'

It was at that time, it all slowly started to make sense to me, and what was going on in my life, but I was still not completely convinced. It was time for me to go undercover for myself; I had to get to the bottom of it all.

After a heavy discussion with Beth and my family, we all began to realize, that except for the first attempt on my life (provided the driver didn't give my license plate number to his mob friends) all of the attempts were away from the house, and this led us to believe no one from the mob must have known where we lived or anything about my family. This was common sense to us otherwise attempts would have been made on their lives or at the house. It was time for me to take things into my own hands before anything else happened to my family or me.

We all agreed Beth and children had to move out of the house; they moved in with one of her girlfriend's. That was the first move we had to make. I couldn't believe they didn't make any attempts on Beth life. I could only hope Vinnie didn't know where Beth moved to and the fact that she had gotten married to me. I explained to Beth I had to take some type of action before we ended up dead. At first, Beth, wanted me to let the police handle it, but knew I would go insane waiting, so she agreed with me.

After all this drama, I went into town, looked for the largest makeup and costume design store I could find in Philadelphia. Once inside, I spent hours, I searched the entire shop for the right look for me.

The store was actually fun; some people held masks over their faces while their friends laughed. In the back of the store little smoke machines operated that filled one section up with smoke. The entire time I was in the store, scary music played throughout the store from its sound system. It reminded me of Halloween.

I placed the supplies on the counter and listened while the register beeped with every item scanned.

"Your total is one hundred, sixty dollars," the check out girl said.

I handed her the money, and grabbed the newly filled bag.

"Have a great night," I said as I exited the store.

Then for my next move, I checked into the hotel around the Philadelphia Airport, where I began my transition into a new person. I used the supplies I purchased and began to alter my appearance and then work on my identification cards.

At last, I thought it was time for me to move on to the Los Angeles area. My first real test would be at the airport, would my new identification work?

"Yes!" I said as I boarded the plane.

My confidence level became heightened and I felt the journey had begun.

CHAPTER 8
FIRST CONTACT!

Now it was time to make first contact. With all the investigating I have done on Brassy, I've noticed he made contact with my old friend Vinnie about once a month. The other man that was with Brassy during our scuffle that day in the college restroom was also in town, and the two of them seemed to meet on a daily basis, at least three or four hours a day.

Before I could make contact with Vinnie, it was time to see if my changed identity was good enough not to be recognized by Brassy.

My first step was to enter the strip club that he seemed to manage. As I walked into the club the first thing I saw was this huge metal detector. It was type of thing that looked like it belonged at an airport. As people walked through it and the machine went off, those people were pulled aside and were asked to remove all the contents from their pockets.

To the customer in front of me I said, "Who the hell are we going to watch, some strippers or the damn president of the United States?"

He said, "Two years ago there was an assassination in here and this machine has been here ever since."

At that moment, I slowly backed up and started to walk back to my car. I knew I would never have made it through the machine with my pistol under my arm.

Once in my car I removed the pistol from under my arm and proceeded back in to the strip club. This time I made it past the huge metal detector without a problem. As I walked in the bar I was mesmerized by how this place was designed. The bar had a shape that reminded me of the capital letter "H", with a clear countertop that had round coins molded into it. The outer edges of the bar had stools through out. The remaining area of the bar was the club's main lounge and had about fifty square tables with one chair on each side of the table. Off to the sides there were small rooms with couches in them; that is where for a twenty-dollar bill you would be seated on the couch and have a girl sit down on your lap and grind on your balls for five minutes. That's how the name couch dance was formed.

The time was seven forty-five in the evening on a Tuesday night. The place was only at half its allowable occupancy. This being my first visit to the club, I pulled up a seat at one of the square tables. A waitress walked up to me with a smile that had great sex appeal; it made it very pleasing to start a conversation with her.

"Hello, my name is Sue and I'll be your waitress tonight; may I take your order?" she said in a normal tone.

"Sure Sue, I'll have rum and coke please," I said, with a smile back to her.

"Would you like a lemon or a lime with that?" "A lime please," I said.

She was well built for a woman of her size; she was only five feet five inches tall. She had on a white v- neck sweater and wore tight, black jeans that had great impact on her ass as she walked away from me.

When Sue approached the table with my drink she said, "Here you go."

Just then I interrupted her and said, "Frank, Frank is my name."

"Okay, here you go, Frank."

"Thank you," I said handing her a five-dollar bill. "Your total comes to four dollars," she said with smile.

I glanced at her smiling and said, "I'm sure you hear this all the time, but you have a very sexy smile; keep the change."

She just smiled and walked away.

Seated at the table, I began to look around the room. I first spotted Brassy seated on the end seat of the stage; continuing my surveillance, I then looked across the stage to where there was a stripper doing her dance. She was a tall woman with long, black hair; she wore a silver thong and fondled her firm breasts for all the men seated around the stage. The more she played around with them, the faster the dollars bills just seemed to flow onto the stage.

When I turned my head back to Brassy's area, I noticed he was in deep conversation with a man in the seat next to him. As I waited for a closer stool the wait seemed like hours.

Finally two seats over from Brassy a man proceeded to get up; with his stool now vacant, it was the true test that I waited for, to see if Brassy would remember me from Philly.

After I sat down I asked, "Could one of you two pass the ashtray?"

Just then the two stopped their conversation and Brassy stared directly at my face. After a long, intense stare Brassy said, "Sure."

Passing the ashtray to the man next to him, he passed it to me.

"Thank you," I said. Brassy just tilts his head as if to say you're welcome without having to verbalize the words.

It seemed Brassy didn't recognize me, and knowing that fact, allowed my body to calm down a bit, especially after all the time I waited and wondered.

As I sat there with this overwhelming feeling inside me, I still felt my plan was going to work.

I finished my drink, stood up and tapped Brassy on the shoulder; as I left the bar I said, "Thanks again for the ashtray."

Although everything went well in the strip club, I knew I had to take these assholes out. I just didn't want to take a chance that one-day Brassy or the other man (whose name I still didn't know) would remember me. Where would I pop these bastards? And when should I do them; should I do them together or at a different time and at a different place? Not sure, I just keep my eye on them and let them slowly get used to seeing me, but not getting too close.

I'd become very visible at the strip club. It had been two months now since I started staking out the club and kept my eyes on Brassy and his partner, who, by the way, finally had a name, Tony. These two men seem to get together every day for lunch and then would meet at the end of the night at the club for drinks. It was very evident with all the envelopes they handled that they were part of Vinnie's mob family. My decision to take these two men out was carefully planned. I decided I was going to pop them at lunch and I was going to pop them both at the same time. My plan was simple and needed to be completed quickly to avoid the local cops or any of the other men from Vinnie's family. To do this, after the hit, I would be assuming my normal look. Why not? After Brassy and Tony were   gone, Vinnie would be the only one who knew what I looked like; that was twenty some years ago.

Today was the right day. It just felt lucky to me so I removed two of my thirty-eight calibers pistols from my closet. Both pistols were special to me because they had been customized not to hold my fingerprint. That was achieved by installing foam grips on the handles and on the triggers.

I waited for Brassy and Tony outside a small café; the two of them where inside enjoying what would become their last lunch. I wanted to get them off guard so I waited for them to be about halfway finished with their meals. I then walked into the café, approached the table with a pistol in each hand, and at point blank range, shot them both at the same time right between the eyes. I shot Brassy with one pistol and Tony with the other. I dropped both pistols right there at the murder scene, turned around, and with a fast pace walked out of the café. I didn't look up, or at, anyone.

Once back at my apartment I removed my disguise, and poured myself a stiff drink to calm me down, after all this was my first killing and my whole body was shaking. I was nervous and scared.

As I stood in front of the bathroom mirror I said to my reflection, "I can't believe you fuck'n did it."

CHAPTER 9
THE MEETING!

It was time for me to meet my old buddy Vinnie. This task was going to be very difficult to do with the news media always surrounding him every time he left his house. I tried to watch Vinnie in his home in order to plan a way to meet with him and get to the bottom of all this shit I've been going through.

I wanted to explore his house so I could get familiar with the layout of his large home. Then, I would be able to decide where and how I could meet my old friend. The longer I observed Vinnie, the more I realized how much of a huge asshole he became. After all these years, all I wanted to ask him was why he has been trying to take me out.

It had been two days now that I've been staking out Vinnie's house and it made me notice how crazy the news media really can be when they think there is a story. I also thought it was pretty funny, and at times it can also be very entertaining to watch what the reporters will actually do to get a story.

Just then, Vinnie walked out of his house and stood alongside this huge, black limousine. It was parked in a half-circle type driveway just outside his front door. The small breeze from the wind made the hot summer day more bearable. As he stood there in a dark-blue, pinstripe, three-piece suit staring at the media, his driver opened the back passenger door, and a beautiful blonde exited the house. She wore a skin-tight, silk, blue dress and proceeded to get into the car. Once in the car, she slid across the back seat very slowly; Vinnie followed her in.

At the last second, Vinnie raised his hand and flicked the media his middle finger saying, "Fuck you." Vinnie lowered his hand as the driver closed the door behind him. With all the windows closed the limousine exited out of the driveway. Just then, the news media scurried to their cars in an effort to arrive at the courthouse before Vinnie's arrival, this left me in my hiding place, alone with Vinnie's empty house.

I tiptoed my way to the back door, and picked the lock; it seemed very easy for me. All the years of helping students and faculty members who forgot their keys or locked their keys in their office had paid off.

When I entered the house, a squeaking noise came from the floorboards as my weight was applied. I began to realize that Vinnie's house was big. As I walked through the place I realized it was going to take more time then I thought, but time was not on my side so I would have to be quick. After I glimpsed through the house, the room Vinnie spent the majority of his time in was very obvious to me from the inside. Although in, my observation from the outside, this room was just a window with a light on.

This would be the place for me to meet with Vinnie. I wanted my entrance to be a surprise. I decided to enter the house from the second floor, hoping the bodyguards wouldn't expect something like that as much as they would a first floor break in.

I would have to climb to the window from the outside. My view from the inside, allowed me to see the window was actually a Dutch door that opens out onto a little window ledge that was designed to let someone stand on. Surrounded by a cement rail with a small gap between the cement base and the railing, this was not just a window as I first thought. Although, this was perfect for me I would have to leave the door unlocked, and then had to pray no one would notice it; that was a risk I had to take.

That night I started toward the house. Sounds were heard as someone approached me in the yard while I creped my way to the house. Those noises made me climb the nearest tree to its first limb. I observed a soldier who was alone, so I jumped down with my hands in an interlocking fashion and I hit him in the head on the way down using that momentum for extra power and knocked him out. This worked for me and gave me the confidence I needed to go through with my entire plan. As I continued my way alongside the house I stopped and stood under the small balcony, everything was quiet. It was so quiet that if I were to throw my rope up with a grappling hook attached to it would make entirely too much noise, so I had to think fast and approach this obstacle without freaking out.

I pulled out a small ball of string from my bag; I began to tie the string to the opposite end of the rope that the grappling hook was attached to. I threw up the small ball of string onto the landing, I heard it land and it began to roll across the window ledge towards the edge. It then rolled under the rail and off the edge of the landing in front of me. As I began to pull the string I stared at it as it started to pull up the rope until the rope went all the way around the railing and then came back down again.

Then I was able to pull the rope very slowly until the hook was in a perfect position without making any noise. I left my bag on the ground in the flowerbed as I climbed up the rope and stood on the small landing. I then checked my pistol, which was a 380. Caliber semiautomatic, the sound of a cricket began to broadcast in the background as I opened the door very slowly.

I walked in and said "Aaa, Vinnie, I hear your searching for me."

As he looked at me in amazement he screamed, "Who the fuck are you? What the hell are you doing in my fuck'n house?"

Just then two bodyguards entered the room.

"Don't fuck'n move or he's a dead man," I shouted. "Take it easy," Vinnie said to his men as he picked up the television remote to lower the volume.

"What the fuck do you want? Money?" Vinnie screamed, with his temper starting to flare to the point the vein in his forehead began to throb.

"It's me, Frank. Take a good look, Vinnie, do you remember me?" I asked.

"It's been a long time, Frank, hasn't it? How long has it been? Twenty-five years?" he asked.

"More like twenty-three" I responded.

"Well what the fuck brings you here after all these years?" he asked. "You do, Vinnie.

Why are you trying to take me out?" I asked. "I don't know what you mean!" he replied.

"Don't play stupid with me Vinnie, after all we been through, I think you can level with me," I replied

"Okay, Frank. You and Beth are the only people left on this goddamn planet to see a murder by me and I was just covering my ass. I will say one thing, Frank, you have brass balls to make it this far. Now why are you here? To take me out?" he asked.

"Well twenty-three years ago, back in that alley, it was a tough situation for you Vinnie. We were young and scared I made a promise to you and kept it. You gave me the chance to live that night in the alley, so I will do the same for you tonight, if you do me one favor," I said.

"And what's that?" he asked.

"You promise to call off your people and let me live in peace, I will let you live and stick to my old promise I gave to you twenty-three years ago. How many more people have to die, Vinnie?" I said.

"Okay, Frank lets start with you putting down the gun and have a drink. Is it still rum and coke after all these years?" he said walking to the small bar in the corner of the room.

After a careful glance over to his bodyguards and trusting my gut feeling about Vinnie, I put the pistol back in its holster under my arm.

"Yes it is, and make it a double, Vinnie," I said.

Vinnie handed me my drink and then sat in his favorite seat with his drink.

"You two can wait outside the doors in the hallway," he said waving his hands as to say get out to his people in the room.

"Have a seat, Frank," he said.

"Sure why not?" I said as I began to feel a little more relaxed, but making sure I still stayed on my guard.

"It's been a long time since we had a drink together. So what have you been up to all these years?" Vinnie said with a big smile.

As I finished my drink I asked, "Can I have another drink?"

I tried to hide my nervousness from Vinnie. "Sure," he said.

After he completed my refill, Vinnie handed the new drink to me and I said, "Vinnie, my life is my life and I just want to live it in peace. Right now I'm here to inform you that you don't have to worry about me. If I can leave here tonight in peace, you will never have to worry about me or Beth. Just as I promised you a long time ago, but if you want to do things the hard way, the next time I will take you the hell out without hesitation."

I removed the replenished glass from Vinnie's hand and sipped some of the drink.

"Well, Frank, being as you made it this far, I will take you seriously." I placed my half empty drink on the table and said to Vinnie, "Do I need to leave out the window as enemies or by the front door, still as friends?"

"Friends, as a friend," Vinnie said, as he opened the door so his men could come back in the room.

"We worked out our concerns and I want you two guys to walk this man to his car."

"Yes, Sir," one of Vinnie's men said.

As I started out the door I saw Vinnie's reflection in the mirror. From behind my back, he signaled to one of his men. By running his thumb across his neck from right to left as to give his man a sign to kill me.

I began to sweat again, but kept my cool as I said to the guards, "This is a nice house," as they walked me out the front door.

"Where is your car?" the man on my left side asked.

"Off the property and up the street," I responded.

"Let's take the car," he said.

"Sure why not?" I asked as the two men began to separate, one opened the door for me and the other walked in the direction of the driver's door on the other side of the car.

This would have to be my escape. Because of what Vinnie had done through the mirror, I knew I wasn't going to make it to my car.

When one of the men started to open the door for me, I kneed him in the groin and grabbed his gun from under his arm. As he began to collapse to the ground, I pointed the gun over the roof of the car at the man who walked for the drivers' door; he fumbled as he tried to pull out his pistol, and I shot him dead between the eyes.

Spinning back towards the man on the ground, I reached down and grabbed him by his collar and whispered, "Tell Vinnie that he really fucked up now. The police and news media will be the last thing he will have to worry about. There is no place he can hide that I will not find him, and tell him I said he is a dead man."

As I whacked him across the face with his owngun, he was knocked unconscious.

Not wanting to press my luck that night I didn't go back in the house after Vinnie. I thought without a plan it could be a mistake, so I released the unconscious man's collar, and let him drop to the ground. I just took off running to the street, away from the house and towards my car.

CHAPTER 10
THE AFTERMATH!

As I arrived at my car, I could feel the adrenaline as it ran through my entire body; it felt like my heart was going to explode. After I inserted the key into my ignition I pulled the driver door closed, turned the key, and drove down the road as fast as I could. When I sped past the driveway entrance, I noticed the first bodyguard that I jumped on from the tree limb was now conscious and approaching the dead driver alongside the parked vehicle in the driveway.

Driving in L.A. for what seem to be hours, I finally arrived at a well known hotel, and parked the car. I still felt the tension in my body; I rested my head on the steering wheel as the sweat dripped onto the steering wheel from my checks and chin. It was as that moment I knew the only thing that was going to calm me down was to stop thinking about what I had just been through. At a steady pace I approached the front doors of the hotel. As they automatically opened, I continued towards the main lobby; I felt the cool air from the hotel's air conditioning system as it touched my wet face, and it sent chills through my body giving me goose bumps.

The hotel lobby was decorated very nice, it was one hell of a spot. Shiny, brass light fixtures were everywhere. High ceilings, cushioned furniture, and the front desk area, which was full of people lined up to check in. Sounds of people's voices and the noise of credit cards being swept through the machines filled the air. Once I strolled through the lobby, I gazed at everything I passed until I walked into the lounge, and with the tension slowly beginning to leave my body, I sat down at the bar.

Waiting for the bartender to finish tending on one of his customers, I lit up a smoke.

"May I help you sir?" The bartender said with a smile.

He was a young man dressed in black pants with a white shirt and a black bow tie.

"It has been one hell of a day. Could I have a rum and coke with a twist of lime please?" I asked.

"Sure thing."

The sound of ice cubes being dropped in the glass could be heard as I blew out the match I used to light my cigarette and tossed it into the nice, clean ashtray. Smoke filled the air around me as I laid my cigarette in the ashtray.

"Here you go sir," the bartender said with a smile as he rushed away to another customer a few seats away.

Just as I took a sip of my drink, a drop of water dripped onto the bar from the condensation that began to form on my glass. Nervously, I kept my eyes on the lounge entrance, I noticed this lovely looking woman walk into the lounge. After a brief look around the lounge her eyes made contact with mine. It was at that moment I gave her a slight smile and a small nod with my head. I lowered my head, picked up my cigarette, and took a long, much-needed drag.

The smoke in the air around me suddenly was replaced with a perfume aroma.

"You look lonely," the woman said as she stopped at my seat.

"Just trying to relax,"I said looking her straight in the eyes.

"Would you like someone to talk to?" she asked. "Sure, why not?"

"So, what, are you here on business?" she asked.

"I guess you could call it business. What about you? Do you live around here or here for business?" I asked.

"I live on the east coast. I'm here on business as well." she replied.

After we both had a few more drinks, things started to heat up a little as she put her warm hand on my damp face and giving me a nice kiss on the lips. Her tongue entered my mouth for a brief second, and then she pulled it away.

"I've been in this town for almost a week now, but you're really the first person I have spoken with that wasn't about business." she whispered after the steamy kiss.

"Too much work and not enough play isn't good," I said with a smile, still thinking about her kiss.

"I was hoping to have a little sex before I left the west coast," she said grabbing the knot of my tie and lowering her hand down the length of it until she felt

something down by my hip.

"Is that a gun or are you just happy to see me?" she asked.

Laughing I said, "Don't freak out, but it is a gun.

However, I'm still happy to see you."

She placed her hand on the pistol and said, "Holy shit, are you a cop or something?"

"Lets just go with 'or something' for now, okay?"

She removed her warm hand from the pistol and placed it back on my now dry face and she stated, "You know this is the first time I met a man with a gun and it is a complete turn on. I thought sex wasn't going to happen for me on this trip, but right now I'm so excited, I feel like screwing you right here. What do you think, should we go up to my room?"

"After all this talk you never told me your name!" I said.

"Oh my god you're right, my name is Lisa Winters; what is your name?"

"It's Frank Mason," I said smiling.

"Lisa, I think it would be a fabulous time for both of us if we were to go up to your room," I whispered back as I gave her a quick peck on the lips. Just then her black heels left the bar chair and landed firmly on the floor as she stood up.

When the bar tender approached, I asked, "Could I have the check please?"

"Yes, Sir," he said promptly, and seconds later handed me the bar bill. I reached into my pocket and pulled out a fifty-dollar bill.

"Keep the change," I said as I walked away with Lisa. "Excuse me," I said to the man I bumped into on

my way to elevator. As we approached the elevator I reached out and pushed the 'up' button on the wall.

Lisa grabbed my left hand firmly with her two hands, pushed them towards the ground just a little and leaned over and kissed me on the lips as we waited for the elevator doors to open.

The elevator door opened and it was empty; entering the elevator, the doors closed behind us.

"Push number five," Lisa said.

I reached out and pushed number five and watched as the needle above the elevator doors go from 'L' to the fifth floor.

Lisa asked me, as she laid her hand on the outside of my suit jacket grabbing my pistol, "Why are you carrying a gun any way?"

"Mainly for protection," I responded.

"Why, are you in trouble or something?" she asked. "I really can't discuss it with you or anyone else,"
I said as the elevator door opened onto the fifth floor.

As we were leaving the elevator, I asked, "What room are you in?"

"I'm in room 512," she said with a smile on her face.

Lisa pulled the door key out of her jacket pocket, slid it into the door, and opened it. Swinging the door open wide, she walked into her room as I followed behind her.

"Would you like another drink, Frank?"

"Sure, if you don't mind, I'll make it. What about you?" I asked.

"A smoke would taste good about now," Lisa said reaching into her pocket pulling out a pack of cigarettes.

She removed one from the pack and put it in her mouth. I lit a match and proceeded to light her cigarette.

"Thank you," she said.

Removing the ice cubes from the bucket, they were cold and wet. She filled it before she left earlier and it was melting. I watched intently as the water dripped between my fingers while I held the ice cubes above the bucket before putting them in the glass. Lisa, with 'sex' in her every step, walked over to the open curtains and slowly pulled them closed; her eyes focused deeply on mine. With the drapes now closed. She reached her hand to the top button of her suit jacket and slowly started to unbutton it. While I took a sip of my drink, she laid her cigarette in an ashtray. With her suit jacket completely unbuttoned, she slid it off her shoulders, removing it completely. She reached into the closet and grabbed a hanger, carefully placing the jacket on the hanger; she hung it in the closet.

She walked over to me. Looking at her white silk blouse, her excitement was very noticeable, with her rock-hard nipples as they darted through the blouse.

I asked, "Are your nipples always that hard and pointed or are you turned on?"

She placed her arms around my neck, and after she kissed me with some heated passion, looked straight into my eyes and said, "Shut up and get in this bed."

Leaning back, she pulled me onto the bed with her.

Meanwhile, back at Vinnie's house, he was at his private bar making a drink in the room that we met in. He was completely outraged; he continued to yell at his people.

Shouting to his men, "How the fuck can this one mother fucker take out four of my men, break the hell into my house, have a conversation with me, and walk the fuck out without a mark? I want you to gather more of our men and get this fucker. I want him dead, fuck'n dead before he leaves L.A. Do you hear me?" he asked turning to the man that I left unconscious on the ground, who now stood in front of Vinnie holding a cold rag on his head.

With Vinnie's temper getting the best of him, he threw his drink across the room hitting the wall, and breaking the glass into pieces, pouring the contents over the wall.

Vinnie said, "Call our cop friends and find out where Frank is and take him the fuck out. I don't care what it takes just make it happen; capeesh?"

"Yes, Sir," the man answered as he picked up the phone.

CHAPTER 11
THE FIREFIGHT!

After a few hours had gone by, the telephone back at Vinnie's house began to ring.

On the fourth ring, one of Vinnie's men named Rocco, picked up the black telephone in the living room, and said, "Speak to me."

The time now is about 8:30 a.m., in the morning hours after my talk with Vinnie.

Rocco was a big man in every aspect. He was tall, fat, and always had a cigar in his mouth. He removed the cigar from his mouth and flicked the ash into an ashtray as he listened to the person on the other end of the phone.

"Okay, okay, hold on a minute, I'll get him," Rocco said as he waddled through the house, in the direction of Vinnie's private bathroom.

Still very pissed off, Vinnie was in the shower trying to calm himself down.

From the shower Vinnie yelled, "What the hell is it?"

"Boss, I think you should hear this," Rocco said as he puffed on his cigar.

"Fuck," Vinnie said as he reached over to the water faucet and shut the water off.

As he opened the shower's glass door Vinnie stepped out and the steam followed him. Vinnie grabbed a towel and began to dry off. He wrapped the towel around his waist, and picked up the phone in the bathroom. "Yeah what is it?"

"Are you sure?" Vinnie said to the man on the other end of the phone. "Great, I'll remember you did this for me."

Still with the towel wrapped around his waist, he stormed out of his bedroom and said to Rocco, who, by this time, made his way back in the living room, "Get some men over to the L.A. Marriott, find out what room Frank is in and take him out for good. Now get a move on."

After a great night of lovemaking with Lisa, I found myself lying next to her in the bed she had pulled me into, with my arm around her neck and as my eyes glared at the ceiling. I realized it had been a while since I had any contact with my wife and family. Will I ever be able to see them again? Or with everything that was happening to me, including Lisa, would I change my whole lifestyle and my simple way of life?

I could tell Lisa's feelings towards me after just one night were strong and I began to feel bad because of what had happened between us last night. I have been faithful to my wife up until last night. My feelings for Lisa were strong as well. The two of us just clicked, it was something we both wanted at the time. I was completely alone over here in this lifestyle I created and didn't want to let anyone know that I had a family that could be used as leverage against me.

With me having a major guilt trip in my head, I decided to remove my arm very carefully, so as not to awaken Lisa, and headed into the bathroom for a shower. After my shower I got dressed.

As I reached for my pistol Lisa asked, "Are you alright Frank?"

Just then I reached down and put my hand around her chin, kissed her, and said, "Yes, Lisa, I'm fine, but things are happening to me that I can't explain and I must leave now. I will be back tonight and we can go to dinner if you still want to see me."

Just then Lisa sat up in the king size bed and said, "There is something I need to tell you. It is very complicated and this was not supposed to happen, but I do want you in my life." I put my finger on her lips and said, "Tonight, at dinner, we will talk," and then began to walk towards the door and opening it.

Once outside Lisa's door I stopped, and slowly leaned back on the wall. I began to wonder what I really was going to do tonight. Room service walked by me with a morning breakfast tray in their hands and the hallway air had filled up with a scent of bacon and eggs.

"Good morning, Sir," one of the room service staff said.

"Good morning," I said back with a smile. Still staring at Lisa's door, I pushed the down arrow button. A dinging sound came from the elevator as the doors opened. I slowly walked in and pushed the 'L' button. The doors closed and the elevator started down towards the hotel lobby.

As the elevator doors began to open I saw one of Vinnie's men pointing at me.

"Holy shit!" I said out loud as my hand reached out for the elevator buttons.

At that time, I saw the man I left unconscious on the ground pulled out his pistol from under his jacket, and point it at me. When he pulled the trigger I saw a flash of light from his pistol and I felt a vibration on my arm, just after I was able to push the number two button on the elevator's control panel.

The doors began to close. I could see people in the lobby scurry for cover and screams from the loud noise of the pistol that was recently fired. With the doors completely closed I felt the elevator start to move up, as well as the pain in my arm. Slowly, I looked down and could see the blood on my arm, and where the blood from my wound had sprayed onto the elevator's very clean walls. "Ding" sounds came from the elevator and the doors started to open.

On my short ride up to the second floor I was able to reach under my wounded arm and remove my pistol from its holster and cock it back installing a bullet in the chamber. When the doors opened, I leaned on the control panel in an effort to peek my head out, that movement splattered blood all over the buttons from my bleeding arm.

I made sure the coast was clear, and then, I began to head to the stairwell hoping to get away from Vinnie's men. I could feel the pain and began to pray I wouldn't get weak from my wound. I walked as fast as I could; my shoulder accidentally crashed into a wall fire extinguisher, thus knocking me onto the ground. As I struggled to get up I heard another gunshot from the direction I was heading towards. At that time I looked up in the direction of the sound and there stood Lisa at the stairwell with a gun in her hand, the gun still pointed down the hallway. I turned my head to the other direction; there was one of Vinnie's men lying on the floor, with a gun in his hand. I made it back to my feet and on my way to Lisa. She stood at the stairwell and when I was in her arms reach, I felt her grab me and as she began to help me into the stairwell, closing the stairwell door behind us.

"What the hell are you doing with a gun Lisa?" I asked in a struggling tone.

Just then, Lisa started to remove the stocking from her right leg.

"Shut the hell up and save your strength, Frank," she said as she proceeded to rip off my sleeve and wrap the nylon stocking just above my wound.

"I don't understand," I said.

"Remember this morning when I said I had something to tell you?" Lisa asked.

"Yes."

"Well I'm with the F.B.I.," Lisa replied.

"Oh great, now I have the mob and the Feds after me. Lisa these are bad people and they are unaware you have any connection with me so we need to split up, before they find out there is anything between us. We can talk later tonight."

"Okay Frank, where should I meet up with you?

"A bar called Vinnie's Place. Do you know where it's at?"

"I'll find it," she said.

"Okay, see you about seven o'clock. The alley behind Vinnie's Place is where this all started many years ago and I'll explain everything to you." I said. Giving her a kiss like it was the last one I was going to give anyone, I said, "Go back to your room and stay there until I lead everyone out of the hotel."

"Sure, Frank, but don't you die on me, I still want you in my life." she said as I started down the steps.

Lisa started slowly up the steps towards her room back on the fifth floor.

As I galloped down the steps at a fast pace, one of Vinnie's men entered the stairwell right below me. The blood from the wound in my arm still flowed from the bullet hole, but had slowed down considerably due to the quick first aid given to me from Lisa minutes ago. I jumped on the man from about three steps up as he entered the stairwell, making it very easy for me to wrap my wounded arm around his neck, covering his face with the blood that had spread over my arm. With the impact of my body weight as it landed on his upper body from the steps, it forced us past the doorway, slammed the stairwell door against the back wall. As all this was happening, with my other hand I reached up, placed my gun on his chest and rapidly squeezed the trigger two times. The sound from my gun had been muffled partly, from the noise of the door as it slammed into the wall. Quickly, I placed my feet on the ground, and then just pushed the man to the floor of the stairwell leaving him there, dead. The other man following me from above, stopped, to help his falling comrade.

Finally, I made my way to the parking lot of the hotel; I was completely astounded when my car had no one watching it. After looking at everyone in the parking lot and felt the area was clear, I began to remove the keys from my pocket. Once I had the car started, I reached down, rapidly putting the car in reverse, backed out of my parking spot, then slamming the gear shifter into drive; I pushed the gas pedal to the floor. My tires spun in place, which formed a lot of smoke, and this loud, high-pitched sound filled the air and a scent of burnt rubber followed until the car began to move; I than drove out of the hotel's parking lot as fast as the car would go.

CHAPTER 12
THE FBI!

Lisa made her way out of the hotel very calmly. As she walked through the hotel's lobby she examined how the local police, who now had filled the lobby, handled a crime scene. They continued to place caution tape around some of the crime scene areas.

Once she arrived at the F.B.I. headquarters, Lisa entered the building, and displayed her identification to the desk clerk at the front desk.

The desk clerk said, "Hi, Lisa. The chief asked me to let you know he needs to speak to you as soon as you arrive."

"Okay thanks."

"Hi, Chief; you wanted to see me?" she asked.

"Yes I do, come in and sit down." He said in an angry tone. "What the hell happened last night? You were to approach this Frank guy, slowly let him know who you were, win his confidence and then give us the signal to come up to the room. Do remember what that signal was?" the Chief asked.

"Yes sir," she said.

"Well tell me what it was again, because it didn't happen that way last night. Go ahead, tell me once again," he demanded.

Lisa removed a cigarette from her pocket and slowly placed it in her mouth. With a slight shake in her hands Lisa lit the cigarette, took a puff and blew it out, the move filled the chief's small office up with smoke.

"Okay," Lisa said. "Once in the room I was to light up a smoke with the curtains open allowing Agent Smith and Agent Wilson to know we made it up to the room. After I gained Frank's confidence I would tell him about the agency. If, or when, he agreed to meet with us, I would light up the second smoke again another signal to Agents Smith and Wilson it was time to come up and knock on the door."

Very angry, the chief said, as he waved Agents Smith and Wilson to enter his office, "Then why did you close the curtains after the first cigarette?"

Just then the two agents entered the office, closed the door and sat down.

"I'm sorry," Lisa said.

"Why did you close the curtains?" Agent Wilson asked.

"Chief, it is very hard to explain. We just clicked and the next thing I knew I just wanted him and I just closed the curtains." she said.

"With all the killing going on in this town since his arrival it was a very dumb thing to do. He could have killed you," the chief said.

"I don't believe this," Agent Wilson said very, upset.

"I'm sorry, Tom," Lisa said.

"I've tried to build a relationship with you for a year now and we haven't screwed once. This man Frank, rolls into town, takes out half the mob, and after a few hours, screwed the F.B.I. too. Who is this guy?" Agent Wilson asked.

Lisa started to say, defensively, "He didn't screw the F.B.I., he screwed me."

"Knock it off you two, your personal life doesn't concern me," the chief yelled from his desk.

"So, now what? Agent Smith asked.

"We need to make contact with this Frank fellow again. I need to find out just what the hell is going on between him and the mob. Lisa, because of what happened last night I'm going to have to remove you from this case," the chief said.

Lisa placed her hands on the chief's desk, smiled and said, "You may want to reconsider that, Sir."

"And why is that?" he asked.

"I will be meeting with Frank tonight and he wants to explain everything to me," Lisa stated to the chief.

"I don't believe this," Agent Wilson said as he stormed out of the chief's office.

"This may be the break we need to find out just what the hell is going on between him and the mob. Lisa you're back on the case, but tonight you must wear a wire; I need to hear all he has to say. I need to know what the hell is going on in this town. When and where are you going to meet him?" the chief asked.

"All I know right now is he wants to meet outside a bar called Vinnie's Place, about seven o'clock. That's if he shows up at all," Lisa said.

Thankful that I was able to escape from Vinnie's people in the hotel, I continued to feel a massive throb in my arm. I started to get concerned that in my effort to slow the blood flow down, I was tightening the nylon stocking too much and that was the reason for all the throbbing. I loosened the stocking a bit, but it was not easy. I had to slowly reach down; firmly grasp the nylon stocking, and place one end in my mouth with the other end in my hand, then allow the tension to ease off a little. This helped the throbbing in my arm to dissipate somewhat. I knew I had to find a place to conduct first aid so I began to check out my apartment. I hoped it would not have any signs of Vinnie's people. With the apartment area looking as if the coast was clear, I decided to take the chance, and headed for my apartment door.

Once inside, I breathed a sigh of relief and started for the bathroom medicine cabinet, and snatched a bottle of rum off the table. I placed the bottle on the sink, and I carefully put my right arm in the sink. I slowly started to remove the nylon stocking from my arm and turned on the hot water; after that, I quickly moved my hand over to the cold water handle. I then turned on the cold; just enough to withstand the hot water as it streamed out of the faucet. I carefully cleaned my wound; that gave me more pain and wasn't the prettiest thing to look at.

I opened the medicine cabinet and removed the first aid kit and a bottle of rubbing alcohol, placing all the items on the bathroom sink. After opening the kit, I looked for the tweezers first; once I found them, I placed the tweezers on the edge of the sink so that I could pour rubbing alcohol over the tweezers.

I then picked up the bottle of rum and took three big gulps placing it back on the sink; I could only hope the rum would help with my pain. Grabbing the tweezers, I stuck them in my wound, as I explored it, probing, to remove the bullet that was lodged in my arm.

Finally finding the bullet, using the tweezers I pinched it on both sides and yanked it out. After a quick glance, I dropped the bullet into the sink. Next, I removed the needle and thread and started to sew the wound closed. After the minor surgery on my arm, I picked up the rubbing alcohol and poured the remaining contents completely over the entire wound, and then, wrapped a bandage around it.

As I walked out of the bathroom, I reached in my pocket to flip open my cigarette pack and removed a smoke with my teeth. I placed the pack back in the pocket and removed my matches. Using just one hand, I lit the match by folding one of the matches around the bottom and placing the head of the match on the strike bar. Then using my thumb I slid the match head down the strike bar, lighting the match and then my cigarette. I placed it on the tip of my cigarette. After a couple seconds I blew the match out. Only with my index finger and my thumb I pulled the match off the pack and laid it in the ashtray.

I jumped slightly as I heard the hum of the compressor from the refrigerator as it came on, and a distant noise from the outside. I leaped over to the window, placing my finger on the mini blind and lifting it up. I started to scan for any signs of unwanted guests outside. After I finished my cigarette, and with my neighborhood that still seemed normal, I decided to take a shower and think about how I might explain things to Lisa tonight when we meet.

CHAPTER 13
THE MISTAKE!

That evening, I slowly drove up to Vinnie's Place. I glared out my windshield and stared at the front entrance of the bar as I wondered if the inside had changed any. After twenty-three years, not much seemed to change on the outside.

Suddenly, Lisa walked into my view. Glimpsing up and down her body, I couldn't believe how beautiful she was; I couldn't wait to talk to her.

After twenty-some years, I thought no one really should remember me or recognize me in the bar.

I did one last examination of the clip in my pistol and placed it back into the holster under my right arm; slowly, I took one more look around. Then got out of the car and jogged across the street.

"Hello Lisa," I said smiling happily.

I could hear the noise of cars when they passed by us in the street and voices of people in conversation could be heard as they walked past our location.

Lisa said, "You look good, Frank. How is your arm?"

"The arm, it will be fine. Damn you smell great," I said, as her perfume scent filled the air.

"I wasn't sure if you were going to show up," she said.

"Let's go inside and sit at a table," I said, holding the door with my good arm.

When we walked into the club I noticed it was more of a restaurant now, compared to the drinking bar it use to be twenty-three years ago.

"Two, smoking," I said to the hostess.

"Tell me, Frank, why is the mob after you anyway?"

"Before I tell you any of that, you tell me, are your F.B.I. friends listening?" I asked.

"Yes, Agent Wilson and Agent Smith are outside," she said

"I can't believe she just told him that," Agent Wilson said to his partner as they waited in a van outside.

Both agents had earpieces and anxiously waited to listen to every word Lisa and I said.

"Follow me," the hostess said as we walked behind her.

"Here you go I hope your night is a pleasant one," the hostess said. "Thank you", Lisa said.

"Well, it all started here many years ago. Vinnie and I were close friends in the Marine Corp. Vinnie wasn't shit back then, although, Loretta's family was impressed with how he had done business for them." I said.

"Do you mean Vincent Malone; the Vinnie that is presently the don of the mob family today?" Lisa asked. I smiled and said, "Lisa, back than he wasn't the don, he was just dating Loretta and she started introducing him to the family."

"I can't believe you knew Vinnie when he was nobody to the family, and today, he is the godfather." Lisa said.

"Well I wish he wasn't the godfather, because if he was still just a nobody, I probably wouldn't be going though all of the shit I have been going through," I said. "If you and Vinnie were such good friends, why aren't you with him?" she asked.

"The night Loretta was killed, and Vinnie killed Loretta's murderer in the alley. The alley along the side of this building was the last time I saw Vinnie, up until last night."

"Holy shit did I hear him right?" Agent Wilson asked Agent Smith as they both straightened up in their seats, getting very interested in our conversation.

"Frank, do you mean you saw him kill the murderer of Loretta?" Lisa asked.

"Yes, I did. I promised him I would never say a word for as long as I lived."

Just then the waitress returned and asked, "Would you like something to drink?"

"Sure, I'll have a rum and coke. What about you Lisa?"

"Just a coke for me," she said.

"Okay", the waitress said heading for the bar.

"That makes you an eyewitness to a murder Vinnie committed." Lisa said.

"No shit! That's why he's trying to kill me. I tried to negotiate this matter with him, letting him know I wanted to live my life and not rat on him. He must have decided not to allow the people who he knows witnessed him kill someone, to remain alive." I said.

"Are we getting all this on tape?" the Chief asked Agent Smith over a walkie-talkie.

"Yes, Sir," Smith responded.

"We can put Vinnie Malone behind bars with this witness, so stay calm and don't scare him off. Do I make myself clear to everyone?" the chief firmly said over the walkie-talkie.

"Yes, Sir," Agent Wilson replied.

The waitress arrived back at the table and said, "Here you go, Rum and Coke for you, and a plain Coke for you."

"Thank you," I said.

"I'm sorry, but I have to ask you a question if I may." said the waitress with her eyes focused straight at me. "Sure, go ahead and ask me." I said to her with a big smile.

"Well I was just wondering. Is that you in that picture on the wall?"

I could feel the nervousness come back into my body, and realized meeting here could have been my first real mistake. Just then, I looked up at the picture the young girl had pointed her finger to in a group of small pictures on the wall. As I stared over at the wall I couldn't believe the picture. It was a picture of a group of people as happy as they could be with it a small brass plate that read "In memory of Loretta." A picture that was twenty-three years old with Vinnie, Loretta, Beth and I, with a small group of people behind us, all with big smiles.

In my mind I quickly flashed back to that night, at my farewell party. I could remember the precise moment the picture was taken. I couldn't believe how happy we all were at that point in our young lives. One hour later Loretta would be dead. I turned back to the waitress at our table; she was still there, staring at me, and said, "It looks like me, but that's not me."

As the young girl walked away from our table, I could see her nod her head no to the bartender as he picked up the telephone.

"Hello, Vinnie, you're not going to believe this shit, but I think the guy you're want is sitting here right in front of me," the bartender said into the phone.

Vinnie screams over the telephone, "Don't let that fucker get away, grab some of your boys and take him the fuck out."

"Lisa, I can't understand, with all this shit that's happening to me, somehow you just make me relax, but I think that picture and that bartender just made me tense up all over again. Let's get the hell out of this place." I said.

"Why would you have picked this place?" Lisa asked.

"How in the hell was I to know they had a picture with me in it on the damn wall?"

Lisa and I started for the door when the bartender and three of his boys came after us, one man blocked the door. I started to use my legs as a weapon, with a back kick that connected on the first man's left cheek, and then, while in the air, I swung my right leg over my left leg and hit another man dead center in the nose. The first kick had sent that man flying across the bar, crashing into bottles that stood on shelves mounted on the wall behind the bar, while the second kick stopped the other guy right in his tracks. All he did was grab his nose and dropped to his knees, like a cat I landed on my feet. The bartender swung a baseball bat at me. At the right moment, using my left foot, I kicked dead center between his wrists and the base of the bat. As my foot continued through, the bartender's hands came apart from each other and the bat flew straight up in the air. After the bat did one flip, I caught it and swung the bat into the bartender's head. In just seconds, there were three men on the floor and the fourth guy reached for his gun. That is when Lisa kicked him twice. Once in the family jewels, followed by a back heel kick to the side of his head, which sent him soaring into some tables, that in turn cleared the way to the front door; we both ran out of the bar, over to the car, and climbed in at a record breaking time.

Once inside the car Lisa asked, "Would you like to meet with my chief?"

"I guess I could listen to what he has to say, I'm just not making any promises to you or him," I said as we drove away from the bar.

When we entered the F.B.I. headquarters building, the agent at the front desk said, "Excuse me, Sir."

Lisa interrupted him, "Its okay, he's with me." "That's fine Agent Winters, but not being a member

of the F.B.I., I must ask for all weapons to be checked in if you have any."

Looking at Lisa, I said, "Sure, not a problem."

I removed my pistol from its holster and gently laid it on the countertop.

"Just sign here," the agent said, as he slid a clipboard over to me. After signing the piece of paper,

Lisa and I slowly walked up the stairs and into the chief's office.

"Come in and have a seat, boy. You been busy since you came to L.A. haven't you?" he asked.

"My life was simple. Now it's everything but simple," I replied.

"You sure don't look like a man who can come into town and take out the mob," the chief said.

"I never wanted to do that, it just appears that way," I said.

"What I would like to do with you, is to lock you the hell up and throw away the key, but you have been very careful haven't you? Do you know since you came to town there is not one piece of evidence that could connect you to any of the murders?" he said.

"I'm not a murderer, Chief. I only defended myself against some very bad people," I said.

"Well how about letting me check out your story and your identity?" he asked.

"What's in it for me?"

"If your story checks out, we will help you to get your life back, but you will have to help us to indict Vincent Malone," he said.

"You don't think Vinnie will still be able to come after me even if he is in prison?" I asked.

"We can protect you," the chief said.

"Do you have a piece of paper and a pen?" I asked. The chief dropped a note pad and pen on the table. I then quickly picked up the pen as it rolled across his desk.

"You're a lefty," the chief said. I began to nod my head up and down.

"Here is my real social security number. Check me out," I said putting down the pen and sliding the pad back to the chief.

"Agent Wilson, run this number through the computer please; thank you? And make it quick," he said in a loud tone.

"I can't wait to find out who the hell you are. This should be good," Agent Wilson said as he grabbed the pad from the chief's hand.

"Can I have a smoke while we wait?" I asked.

The chief nodded his head to give me the go ahead. Agent Wilson was in the other room; he anticipates the findings as they began to spit out of the printer.

Agent Wilson walked into the chief's office, "You're not going to believe this, boss. This guy is clean as a whistle. Not even a parking ticket, look."

"I'm impressed, how did you get mixed up in all this shit, Francis?" the chief asked as he scanned the sheet.

"It's Frank, call me Frank, and that's a very good question," I said, as I flicked the ashes of my cigarette into a nearby ashtray.

"This report tells me you have a wife and three children. Where are they now?" the chief asked.

Just then Lisa laid her head face down on top of her hands that were crossed over one another.

"They're in a safe place," I said.

"If you testify against Vinnie, we will put him in jail for a long time. Protection for you and your family is not a problem," the chief said.

"I guess that is the best plan, and the only way for all this shit to stop," I said, crushing my cigarette into the ashtray.

"Fine! Vinnie's trial restarts up in two days at nine o'clock in the morning. We will have to introduce you then as a living witness who will testify as an eyewitness to Vinnie actually committing a murder.

Until that time, we need to put you on ice, to prevent anyone from harming you," the chief said.

"That sounds like a good plan to me. Just give me three hours to gather my belongings and I'll do whatever you think is right," I said.

"I don't know, Frank; we really need you to testify. What if something happens to you and you don't make it back?" the chief asked.

"Don't worry, I'm not the only witness, my wife Beth was there too; I'll be back," I said.

"Wait, wait a minute. Do you mean your wife was an eyewitness too?" The chief asked.

"Yes, Sir, but I want to keep my family out of all this or there is no deal." I said.

"Okay, we will try it your way, but if we need to, we will have to produce her." The chief replied.

CHAPTER 14
THE HIT!

When I arrived back at my apartment I knew I had little time. So I had to remove Vinnie out of the equation in order to keep my family out of this ordeal. I knew this wasn't going to be easy. My gut just kept telling me that until I terminated Vinnie nothing was going to stop.

I began to slowly pack my things that I would need to get my life back, mostly everything was clothing. My military supplies were going to have to stay until the trial was over. As I stood there, I just looked intently over the room, what could I do? I thought to myself, my eyes stopped at this small, metal case with a magnet on the back half of it.

I walked up to the table the case was on, grasped it with both hands, and opened it very slowly. Inside was a small amount of C-4 explosive.

"Perfect," I mumbled to myself as though a light bulb just went off in my head.

I laid that on the same table, the noise from the table was getting louder as my hands started to push things around on the table, searching for the one item I needed.

"Yes," I said aloud when I found it.

It was an electrical timer for the C-4. I grabbed the two devices and my bag of clothing; back to the car I went. Once in my car, I glanced at my watch and calculated how much time I had before I would be missed by the F.B.I., and then, how much time before Vinnie was going to be at the courthouse. I figured about eight twenty five in the morning Vinnie would be in his car and on his way.

I set the timer for the needed time frame. I pushed the small button with my index finger from the off position to the on position; the timer began to count down. Slowly I laid the timer on the car seat next to me; starting my engine, I headed towards Vinnie's house.

It was now dusk outside. Not too light, nor was it too dark for me to plant my farewell gift on Vinnie's car. I parked my car on the roadside just up the street, out of sight from anyone's view presently in the house or on the property. I reached over to the passenger seat, grabbed the C-4, and opened the metal case. Looking at the C-4, I began to smile as I picked up the timer. I shut the timer off carefully, so not to lose my countdown time. I inserted the timer into the C-4. The whole street was silent. I was almost too scared just to open my door, that's how quiet the neighborhood sounded. It made me close my door as softly as I could; then I managed to sneak my way over to Vinnie's big limo parked in the driveway. Still not being seen, I lay down alongside the car and slid myself under it. I turned the timer back on, and resumed my countdown, slowly, I closed the case. I reached up and stuck the case in the most obscure place I could find, and slid out from underneath the car. I quietly made my way back to my car, and drove away.

At last I made it to the F.B.I.'s building; I walked into the Federal Building's entrance with just my bag of clothing. I smiled at the agent seated at the desk.

"Let the chief know that I'm back, with time to spare," I said.

"Sure thing," the agent said as he picked up the telephone.

Minutes later, the Chief walked over to me from the stairway.

"You are doing the right thing, Frank; the best place for Vinnie is behind bars. We will hold you at our safe house or here until the trial. After you testify, we will get you back to your family as soon as we can, okay?" the chief asked.

"Sure, sounds great to me, but let's make it the safe house. I really don't feel like sleeping on your desk," I said.

"Fine, the safe house it will be," the chief said.

They moved me to the safe house without a problem.

Once we were settled there I asked the chief, "Could I speak to Lisa alone for a moment?"

"Just for a few minutes; let's go guys. Let's get some sunshine," he said.

As I stood in the living room alone with her I said, "Lisa, I'm sorry." With one of those woman attitudes Lisa said, "Sure, I bet Frank. What was I; just another notch in your belt?"

"That's not what it was at all," I said

"I fell for you, I wanted you in my life and it turns out you're married and will be leaving after you testify," she said.

"Why can't we still be friends?" I asked.

"In time, maybe we can, but it will take a little time for me to want to meet your family," Lisa said picking up the bread still in the supermarket bag, and throwing it across the kitchen table onto the counter top.

My few minutes with Lisa, were up as the agents opened the door, and reentered the house.

Finally, two days had passed it was time.

"We will go to the office first, and you will wait there until we present our witness proposal. After that, we will come back for you," the chief said. "Whatever you feel is the best way is fine with me."

Outside Vinnie's house, the media was building and somehow found out about a surprise witness. Vinnie walked out of his house and waved to the cameras, headed towards the open door of his limo.

"Vinnie, Vinnie, what do you think of the agency's surprise witness?" one of the broadcasters yelled to him.

Vinnie stopped and said, "I will answer that question. The F.B.I. can say anything they want about their surprise witness. I still say they have no case against me at all."

"Vinnie, Vinnie", someone yelled from the media. "No more questions," he yelled to the crowd as he placed his hand on the roof just before ducking to enter the backseat.

The driver slammed the door closed, and as the media still yelled and screamed for Vinnie, the driver walked around to the driver's door; at a normal pace, he opened the door, sat in the drivers seat, and turned the limo's engine on.

Once inside Vinnie said, "Let's get the hell out of here." "Sure thing, boss," the driver said and began to drive out the driveway. After traveling, about three- quarters of the way down the street, still with all the media cameras on his car, there was a huge boom; the car blew apart. Pieces of the car flew all over the street; many people in the crowd covered their ears from the noise of the explosion. The smell of burning rubber consumed the air, and the crowd was now in a big panic.

Meanwhile, back at the bureau's headquarters, I sat in the chief's office with coffee in my hand.

Agent Wilson walked in and yelled, "Chief, you must come and watch what's happening on the television station, hurry."

We both left the office and walked out to the television area. The media coverage of Vinnie's car as it blew up into a million pieces, with him still in it, was being displayed.

Just then Agent Wilson said, "Okay, that's it, you're under arrest, Frank."

"Hey, how could I of done it you moron, I've been with all of you people for the last two and a half days," I said.

The chief walked up to me and said, "You're good, and you sure know how to cover your ass don't you?"

"I don't have any idea what you're talking about."

"Let him go, Wilson," the chief said as he walked over to me and whispered, "I'm putting your ass on a plane. Go home to your family and get the hell out of my town."

At the airport, I said my goodbyes to the chief, and, to Lisa.

After a small goodbye kiss on Lisa's cheek I said, "When you think we can be friends, call me."

"I'll try Frank," Lisa said, as she took my telephone number that I had written down on a piece of paper from my hand.

As Lisa started to back off, I smiled at the chief and said, "This was fun. Do you think the agency needs help?"

"That will be the day, Frank," he responded back with a little smile "You're right! Maybe I'll look into the private detective business instead," I said, as I boarded the plane for Philadelphia.

"Are you okay, Agent Winters?" the chief asked as they both watched the plane take off.

"Yes, Sir, and in time maybe I will give him a call," she said.

"You know he probably would make a good detective," the chief said as they walked away from the window at the boarding gate.

THE END